THE CHRISTMAS STORY

THE CHRISTMAS STORY
A PICTURE CORGI BOOK 0 552 54937 1

First published in Great Britain by Doubleday,
an imprint of Random House Children's Books

Doubleday edition published 2003
Picture Corgi edition published 2005

1 3 5 7 9 10 8 6 4 2

Copyright © Ian Beck, 2003
Designed by Ian Butterworth

Picture Corgi Books are published by Random House Children's Books,
61–63 Uxbridge Road, London W5 5SA,
a division of The Random House Group Ltd,
in Australia by Random House Australia (Pty) Ltd,
20 Alfred Street, Milsons Point, Sydney, NSW 2061, Australia,
in New Zealand by Random House New Zealand Ltd,
18 Poland Road, Glenfield, Auckland 10, New Zealand,
and in South Africa by Random House (Pty) Ltd,
Endulini, 5A Jubilee Road, Parktown 2193, South Africa

THE RANDOM HOUSE GROUP Limited Reg. No. 954009
www.kidsatrandomhouse.co.uk

A CIP catalogue record for this book is available from the British Library.

Printed in Singapore

For
Roderick Gradidge.

THE
CHRISTMAS
STORY

Ian Beck

PICTURE
CORGI

The story of the birth of Jesus
began in a garden in the city of Nazareth,
where Mary and Joseph lived.

Mary was alone in the garden when an angel,
who was called Gabriel, appeared before her.
"You have been chosen by God," said the angel.
"You will have a very special baby boy, who will
be the Son of God, and you shall call him Jesus."

Mary was of course surprised, but very happy,
and she ran to tell Joseph the amazing news.

Some months later, by order of the government, Mary and Joseph had to travel far away to Bethlehem to be counted. It was a long journey, but their little donkey carried Mary all the way to the city

Bethlehem was very crowded with people who had also come to be counted. Mary knew that her baby would be born soon but there was nowhere to stay.

The innkeepers all shook their heads. "I'm sorry, but there is no room at the inn," they said to Mary and Joseph.

Βut one innkeeper felt sorry for Mary: he could see how tired she was. He said that they could rest in his stable with the animals, where they would be warm and dry.

Far away in the East, three wise men had seen a bright new star in the sky. They knew that this was a sign that a special baby was to be born who would be a King to all mankind. The three wise men set off to follow the star.

The shepherds came to the stable and brought the simple gift of a new lamb for the baby. They knelt in wonder before the manger.

The wise men had followed the star to the stable in
Bethlehem. They brought with them precious gifts for
the baby, of Gold and Frankincense and Myrrh.

The animals in the stable, the oxen,
the cows, the sheep, the doves and the mice,
gathered round the manger, for even they
knew that this was the Son of God.

High above the stable the night sky
was filled with angels, who gave thanks to
God and welcomed the new baby with
their beautiful music.

And now, thousands of years later,
at every Christmas we remember the
marvellous story of how Jesus was born.

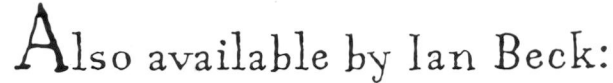

Also available by Ian Beck:

THE LITTLE MERMAID

★

THE TEDDY ROBBER

★

PETER AND THE WOLF

★

THE OWL AND THE PUSSY CAT

★

TOM AND THE ISLAND OF DINOSAURS

★

THE NUTCRACKER
written by Berlie Doherty

★

PUSS IN BOOTS
written by Philip Pullman

★

THE JUMBLIES
written by Edward Lear